FRANKLIN THE FLY

R. O. BLECHMAN

CREATIVE EDITIONS

Library of Congress Cataloging-in-Publication Data
Blechman, R.O., 1930–
Franklin the fly / by R.O. Blechman.
Summary: Franklin, a fly, introduces himself to the
reader, describing what his life is like, and then
makes a friend when he prevents a butterfly
from being captured in a net.
ISBN 978-1-56846-148-9
[1. Flies – Fiction.] I. Title.
PZ7.B6167Fr 2007
[E] – dc22   2006034144
First edition
2 4 6 8 9 7 5 3 1

To Alvin, who said,
"I want you to write a
children's book.
And use color."

Sometimes I think the worst thing in life is to be a little fly in a big city.

... then something else happens.

Like a person squishing you
(although I'm pretty fast, so,
knock on wood, I'm still around).

But I'll tell you something
that's even worse.

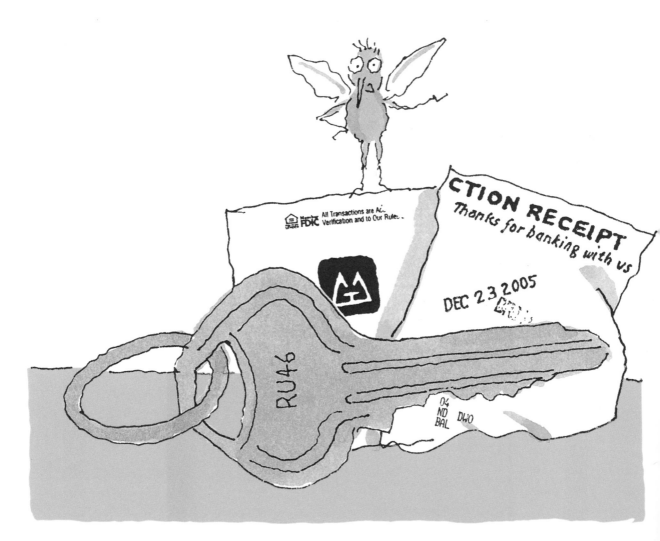

Flypaper.

My Uncle Warren lost almost
his entire family last summer.

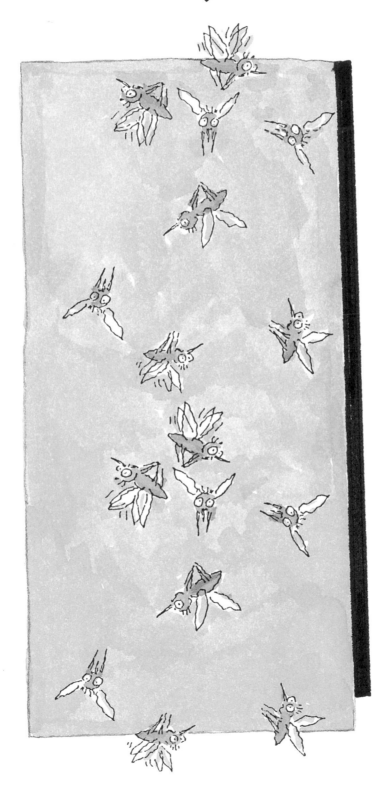

Can you imagine people using
a thing like that? Sticky flypaper?!
So I try to stay away from people ,...

... except when they leave good things lying around their tables. Honey, cookie crumbs, things like that.

But on second thought there are
worse things than being a fly.
For example, a delicious animal.
A pig, say, or a goose or chicken.

There you are, living off the fat of
the land, so to speak, thinking that
life consists of nothing but getting
fatter and fatter, and . . .

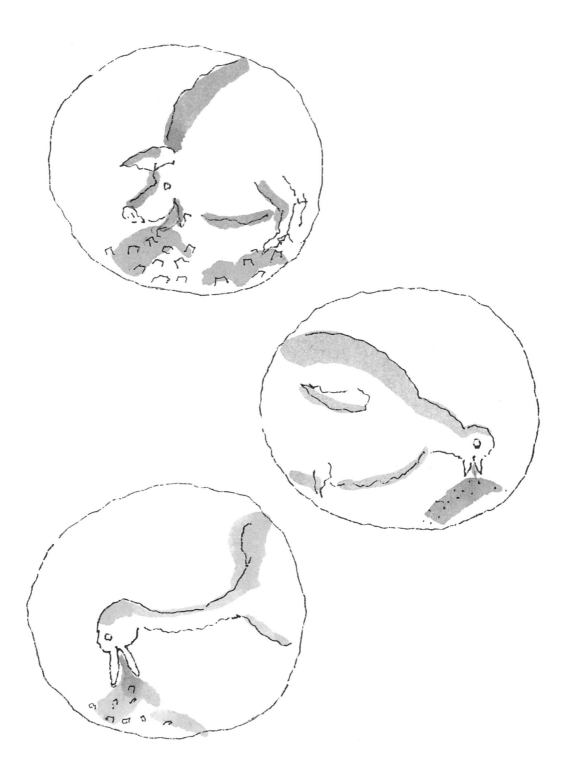

... all you have to do is just lie around, waiting for your next meal, ...

... when suddenly, ...

... *Slice!* ....

... you become
somebody else's
meal!

Now me, I have no expectations.

I play life easy.

For example, I like to leave the city
from time to time.

In the country there aren't many people,
just lots of sunshine and flowers.

I fly around, making circles ...

... and patterns.

When I'm really bored, I do things
I see. Copy them.

Like this.

A face, right?

Or this.

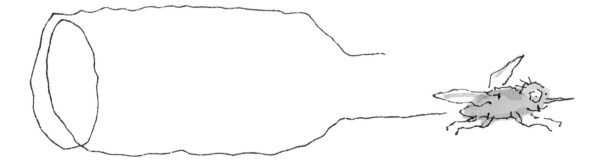

A bottle.

This is an easy one.
It's abstract.

Here's my favorite.
A four-leaf clover.

My friends all think I'm crazy doing stuff like that. "You an artist or something?" they say, but I don't mind.

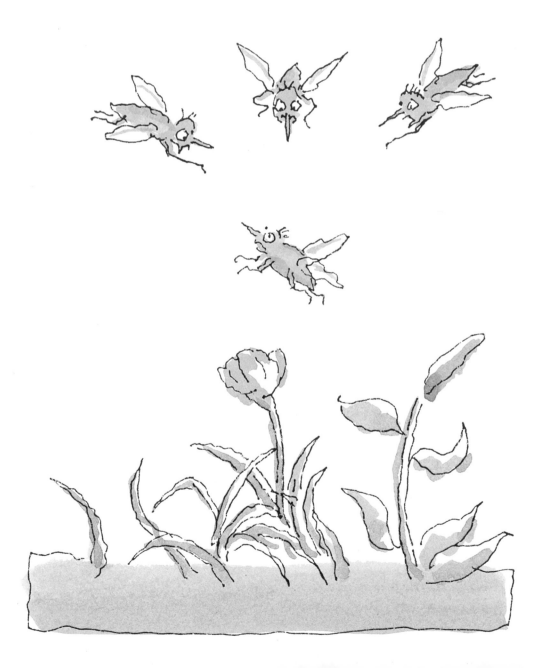

"Sticks and stones...," you know the old saying, "... may break my bones, but words can never hurt me."

I suppose that's not a hundred percent true. For one thing, I don't have any bones, right? And for another, words can hurt. A scratch or a bruise, it can go away in a day or two. But the mind can be like flypaper. Things can stick there forever.

So now you know something about me, and you know I have a pretty nice life, except maybe, sometimes, I do get kind of lonely.

But if that's my worst problem
I can't complain, because think of
flypaper, or tasty animals, or ...

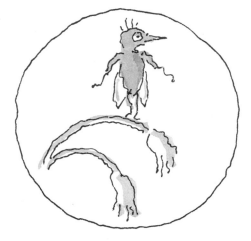

WHOA!

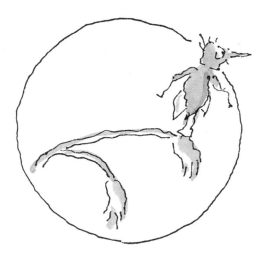

What's that in the field?

It's a person!
With a net!

That butterfly is heading... *"HEY!*
Open your eyes!" ... straight for him.

And he is heading straight for her!

I'll do my Loop-the-Loop ...
and Double Somersault Spring ...

... and my Tickle-Tickle thing
until he drops that net.

He dropped it!

"Oh," the butterfly says
(what a sweet voice she has!)
"I can't thank you enough."

"You don't have to thank me.
But, if you'd like, you can
follow me to some neat places
I know."

So now I have a friend.

Maybe one day I'll tell you more about myself since we're friends too, right?